Majedy Majedy
Always the Queen

Rachel Ruth

Illustrations by Hank Lamlech

In a place not too far away or long ago lived two sisters. Annabelle, the older sister, had joyful cheeks and a sweet disposition and Grace, the wee one, had skinny legs and sparkly eyes. Despite the four years between them, they were best friends.

Now Annabelle could sometimes be bossy, but this didn't seem to bother little Grace, because she knew her older sister was very naive and didn't notice her demanding ways.

It was a day like all other summer days. Annabelle was wearing a frilly dress with picture-perfect bobby socks trimmed in lace and blue matching shoes. She was beautiful in little Grace's eyes. Every morning after breakfast Annabelle would take Grace out into the front yard to play games. By the time the dew burnt off the grass, they were playing Annabelle's favorite game called "Queen." By the front steps, Annabelle sat up tall in a chair looking like she did at church. Her joyful cheeks and beautiful smile made her look regal as she reigned over her front yard kingdom.

"Servant girl, please come here," Annabelle, summoned her servant sister.

Then Grace came scampering out from behind an enormous oak tree in her dingy, hand-me-down dress that had once belonged to her big sister Annabelle.

"Here I am, your Majedy," she said in a mousy voice as she pulled her dress out on each side with her fingers and then bowed and curtsied.

"May I have some tea?" asked Queen Annabelle as she waved her hankie.

On her skinny legs Grace galloped back behind the big oak tree to her imaginary kitchen and prepare her sister's tea. Then she dutifully walked out, with a miniature china cup and saucer for the queen.

"Oh Majedy, Majedy
You're Queen of my day.
Our yard is your land,
your wish my command,
so sit and look pretty
while my skinny legs stand."

"May I have some cake too?" Queen Annabelle inquired.

"Yes, your Majedy," Grace said, as she ran back to her kitchen behind the big oak tree on her tippy toes.

"Oh Majedy Majedy
I bring you tea, cookies,
cake and sometimes cream.
All the while I dream
that you're the servant
and I'm the Queen."

Grace chanted under her breath as she pretended to take a piece of cake and put it on a plate. Then she scampered back out and took her place as the servant girl.

"Your Majedy, here is your cake."

"Can I have some more tea?" requested Annabelle again.

"Yes, your Majedy," said Grace as she went back to her kitchen.

"Oh, servant girl, you forgot my cup," called Queen Annabelle from her throne.

Grace was too smart to wear herself out, so she poked her head out from behind the tree and replied, "I'll bring you a new one, Your Majedy."

All the while, the girls played Queen for what seemed like forever to Grace, but in reality, it only lasted for a few minutes.

That night the girls were fast asleep in their bunk beds when a thunderstorm awoke Annabelle. She heard Grace whimpering from the bottom bunk. Being the motherly type that she was, Annabelle bolted out of bed, but as she was climbing down to check on her little sister she noticed Grace wasn't awake. She was dreaming, so Annabelle laid down on the floor to be close to her and fell back asleep.

The next morning while they were eating breakfast, Annabelle asked her little sister if she'd had a bad dream in the night.

Grace wondered how Annabelle knew about her horrific dream.

"I didn't have a bad dream," she said.

"I heard you crying last night while you were sleeping."

"I didn't dream anything," Grace retorted as she stopped eating and marched over to the couch. There she sat with her arms crossed over her chest, and pushed out her lower lip as she thought about her dream. Smiling to herself she remembered Annabelle was bringing her tea and telling her how pretty she looked. Grace thought she looked pretty good herself, but she could never tell her older sister about her dream or how she wanted to be Queen. What would Annabelle say? Would Annabelle not want to play with her anymore?

Grace's deep and troublesome thoughts were interrupted when she heard Annabelle ask if she wanted to go outside and play.

"Play what?" Grace asked.

"What do you mean?" replied Annabelle.

"I don't want to play today."

"Grace, come back to the table and finish your breakfast," their mother said as she listened to the two girls talk.

"What's wrong with you, Grace? It's not like you to be arguing with your older sister. Are you sick?"

"I just don't want to go out and play."

"We can play inside if you want," consoled Annabelle as she reached out to hold Grace's hand

"Will you paint my fingernails?" Grace asked.

"Sure, what color?" Annabelle replied as Grace got up and followed her into their bedroom.

"I want the orange bottle with the glitters."

As Annabelle painted, Grace squirmed while she daydreamed about being Queen.

"Stop moving or they'll get smudged. Do you want to play after this?"

"Queen?" Grace stuttered under her breath.

"What?" Annabelle asked. "I thought you said you didn't want to go outside."

"I didn't say I wanted to play Queen."

"I heard you say Queen."

"I didn't," screamed Grace.   Their mother poked her head in to see what the screaming was about, but by that time Grace was pouting again and Annabelle was trying to console her.

"You girls really need to stop this bickering. Your baby brother is going down for a nap, so go on outside," she told them in her scolding voice.

Grace's stubborn tendencies made her move in slow motion as she walked past her mother and sister. Annabelle followed her little sister with adoring eyes, because in her heart she felt sorry for making her sister mad.

The fresh air washed away the grumpy feelings Grace was feeling and replaced them with guilty ones. So she went and retrieved the outside lawn chair and set it up for Annabelle to sit in, because she had decided it was okay if they played Queen.

"Oh Majedy Majedy
Let's clear the air,
you can be Queen.
I know the routine, so
let me bow down, and
look at your feet."

Annabelle quickly sat down as she reached up to smooth down her shiny brown hair, and then folded her hands in her lap. Grace watched and wondered why she always wanted to be so prim and proper.

"Servant girl, please stand up," Annabelle ordered.

"Yes, your Majedy," Grace answered as she stood up and pulled down her hand-me-down dress.

"Today, I would like iced tea and a biscuit with grape jelly," Queen Annabelle demanded as she smiled down at her skinny little sister.

"Yes, your Majedy." Grace ran to her imaginary kitchen behind the large tree. She wanted to be gracious, so her sister would play with her all day, but she didn't like to play Queen.

She vowed to herself, that when she got bigger, she would be Queen one day. Just for once, she thought.

"It sure is hot out here. Where are you servant, girl?" Annabelle called.

Grace came running out with her imaginary tray and set it on Queen Annabelle's lap. Then she curtsied and retreated to her kitchen where she sat down on the ground and waited for the next command.

"I'm done now. Please take my tray," called Annabelle again.

"Yes, Your Majedy."

"You spilled the ice out of the glass," Annabelle complained.

"I'm sorry, Your Majedy," Grace said as she plucked imaginary ice cubes off her lap and put on them on her imaginary tray. Then she curtsied and left for the kitchen behind the tree.

"Can we be done now?" Grace asked.

"Sure," Annabelle said as she walked over and put her arm around Grace's shoulder in a motherly way. "Love you, little sis. What do you want to do now?"

"Let's go and get our pop bottle caps and smash them with dad's hammer or go catch caterpillars."

"We can do both, which do you want to do first?" Annabelle asked.

"Pop bottle caps."

So, Grace and Annabelle got their bag of pop bottle caps and hammer and sat down in the front yard by an old tree stump. They began to smash their bottle caps, until Grace got bored and wanted to go look for caterpillars.

Annabelle knew it was too early in the day for caterpillars, but she agreed with what Grace wanted to do. They didn't venture long before their search was quickly thwarted by their mother, calling them in for lunch.

After lunch, the girls were sent to the bedroom they shared for quiet time. Grace as usual had ants-in-her-pants and didn't want to lie on her bottom bunk. So, she repeatedly kicked the bottom of the mattress to the bunk-bed above her knowing that Annabelle was lying up there.

"Stop it," Annabelle said.

"Will you look at books with me?" Grace asked.

"Yes, go pick a book out and climb-up here."

Grace was thrilled and scampered up the ladder with a book in hand. She loved lying on the bed with her big sister and looking at books.

Soon their mother came and told them they could get up. The girls made their way out to the vinyl couch to watch cartoons. Grace decided Annabelle had a better place to sit, and she wanted it. Their mother came in to see what the commotion was about, and found Grace throwing a fit.

"Come with me, Grace," their mother said. "Right now."

Grace knew she was in trouble by the tone of her mother's voice. So, she fell in step behind her until they reached the girls' bedroom.

"What is wrong with you, today? First, this morning and now again. Why are you cranky?" she asked as she smoothed down Grace's hair.

"I don't like playing Queen. I have to play every day, and Annabelle always gets to be Queen."

> "Oh Majedy, Majedy
> Always the Queen,
> day after day.
> Why can't it be me?
> Aren't I pretty enough
> to ever be Queen?"

"Oh, sweetie. You are pretty. You're my little sparkly eyed girl, and I think you're beautiful."

"Really?"

"Absolutely. Sit down here; I want to tell you something, just between you and me. Your sister, Annabelle, loves to play Queen. That's why she wants you to play every day, and you're good to play with her. You know why?" Grace's mother asked her.

"No, why?" Grace asked back.

Grace sat quietly and stared at her mother's hands that were holding hers. She wasn't quite sure what her mother meant as she shrugged her shoulders.

"Do you understand? Who painted your nails this morning, looked at books with you during quiet time, and hunted for caterpillars with you? Who smashed pop bottle caps with you? I think your big sister is awful good to you. Don't you?"

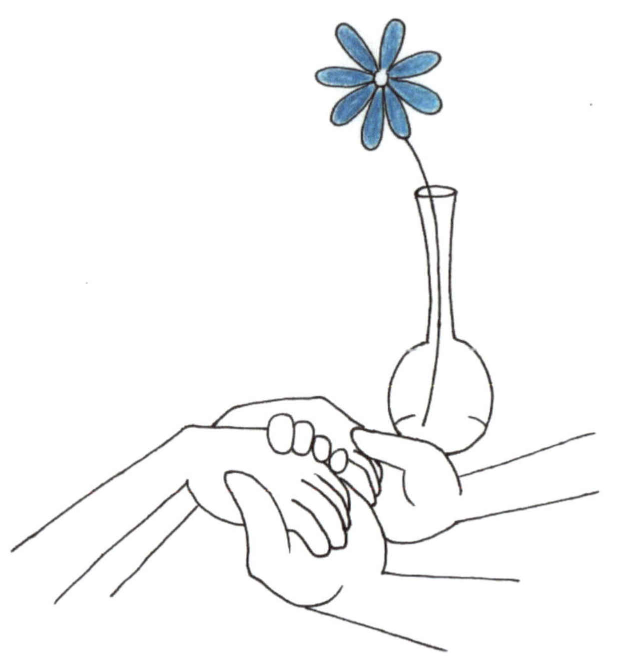

"Yes," Grace conceded.

"She only wants to be Queen for a few minutes, and that's why she wants to play that game. So maybe, you should think about this, and even think of some nice things you can do for Annabelle throughout the day, because she sure does pamper you."

Grace smiled up at her mother, not because she felt like a Queen but because she had a new understanding for her big sister, Annabelle.

"Oh Majedy Majedy
In my mommy's eyes I see,
that all day long
I am the Queen.
So, just for a minute
Annabelle wants to be."

THE END

Rachel Ruth

The moral of the story is:
In every little girl
there lives a Queen,
whose beauty is more
than just skin deep.
So let her shine,
and watch her grow
so all the world
can see her glow.

A special thanks to Rebecca Brower - Conceptional Inspiration
Hank Lamlech - Illustrations, Fawn Martz - Graphic Design,
Theresa Lacey – Copy Editing, , Michael Ilacqua – Cover design
and John O'Melveny Woods, my Publisher.